Ring-
Mon

Save our Swamp

Scholastic Children's Books
Scholastic Publications Ltd
7-9 Pratt Street, London NW1 0AE, UK

Scholastic Inc
730 Broadway, New York, NY 10003, USA

Scholastic Canada Ltd
123 Newkirk Road, Richmond Hill
Ontario, Canada L4C 3G5

Ashton Scholastic Pty Ltd
PO Box 579, Gosford, New South Wales
Australia

Ashton Scholastic Ltd
Private Bag 1, Penrose, Auckland
New Zealand

First published by Scholastic Publications Ltd, 1993
Copyright © Frank Rodgers, 1993

ISBN: 0590 55312 7

Typeset by Rapid Reprographics, London

Printed and bound in Belgium by Proost Book Production.

10 9 8 7 6 5 4 3 2 1

Ring-tailed Monster

in
Save our Swamp

Frank Rodgers

Hippo

The Monster Swamp was a quiet, peaceful, and secret place. It had been the Monsters' home for a very long time.

One morning Ring-tailed Monster looked out of
her mud-mound and smiled. "Ah," she said,
"another lovely, quiet day."

Actually it wasn't really quiet. The Monsters
were singing and laughing, birds were whistling
and small animals were chattering. But it was
the kind of noise that Monsters liked...no cars,
TV sets or stereos.

Ring-tailed Monster loved nature and liked to wander through the swamp talking to the birds, insects and animals.

They liked Ring-tailed Monster too and always told her all the latest swamp news...which families were building new homes, which were having babies and which ones had just moved into the swamp.

That morning Ring-tailed Monster was introduced to a new arrival – the Pink Pyjama Bird.

"Pleased to meet you," said Ring-tailed Monster. "Excuse me not getting up," said Pink Pyjama Bird, "but I'm sitting on my eggs."

Ring-tailed Monster smiled. "Will they hatch soon?" she asked.

She didn't hear Pink Pyjama Bird's reply however, because all of a sudden there was a tremendous roar from the edge of the swamp.

The animals were terrified.

"It must be the Wild Monsters!" they cried.
"Run! Hide!"
Everyone scattered.

Ring-tailed Monster heard the roaring noise
again.

"That doesn't sound like the Wild Monsters,"
she thought. Bravely she crept out and peeped
through the leaves to see what it was.

Coming slowly across the swamp towards her
was a huge bulldozer. It knocked down and
crushed everything in its path as it prepared the
way for a new road.

"Oh!" gasped Ring-tailed Monster. "That thing is flattening the swamp! We're all in danger!"

Frantically she rushed away to warn the animals.

"Can't stay here!" she cried. "You'll be flattened! Come with me!" And she led everyone away from the bulldozer to safety towards the Monsters' mud-mounds.

But when they got there Hairy Monster told
them that he had seen the bulldozer too... and
the mud-mounds were right in its path!

"Means we'll have to leave!" said Curly-top Monster.

"Leave?" exclaimed Lesser-spotted Monster. "But this is home! All live here! We must save our swamp!"

"Perhaps we should talk to the bulldozer," suggested Furry Monster. "Ask it nicely to go away."

Hairy Monster shook his head. "I don't think it would," he said. "It looks more bad-tempered than the Wild Monsters."

Just then Ring-tailed Monster gave a shout.
"Where's Pink Pyjama Bird?" she cried.

The animals gasped. They had forgotten about
the new arrival in all the excitement.
"Got to save it!" cried Ring-tailed Monster.
"Going to get flattened!"

"So will you!" shouted the Monsters as Ring-tailed Monster rushed off. "Be careful!"

When Ring-tailed Monster got to Pink Pyjama
Bird's tree the bulldozer had almost reached it.
The ground shook as the giant machine
lumbered nearer and nearer.

Ring-tailed Monster called to the Pink Pyjama
Bird as loudly as she could. "Come down!" she
cried. "Give me your eggs. I will carry them!"

Pink Pyjama Bird looked down. "I'm staying here," she said. "My babies will hatch soon." "But what about the bulldozer?" wailed Ring-tailed Monster. "You'll get flattened!"

Pink Pyjama Bird waved her wings. "But the
bulldozer has stopped!" she said.
Ring-tailed Monster looked. It was true.
The bulldozer *had* stopped.

Not only that, the people in the bulldozer were watching and listening. "That's a Pink Pyjama Bird!" they cried in amazement. "The rarest bird in the world!"

"We can't flatten the swamp where the Pink
Pyjama Bird lives," they said. "It wouldn't be
right. We'll just have to build the road
somewhere else!"

So the bulldozer turned round and trundled away, never to be seen again.

"Hooray for Ring-tailed Monster and Pink Pyjama Bird!" cheered the Monsters. "Our swamp is saved!"

The Monsters were so delighted about not
having to leave their swamp after all that they
had a big party.

All the animals, birds and insects were invited.
And the guests-of-honour of course, were Ring-
tailed Monster...

and Pink Pyjama Bird and her four newly-hatched Pink Pyjama chicks.